C. Cashmore

Artificial Incubation

C. Cashmore

Artificial Incubation

ISBN/EAN: 9783337380625

Printed in Europe, USA, Canada, Australia, Japan

Cover: Foto ©Andreas Hilbeck / pixelio.de

More available books at **www.hansebooks.com**

Artificial Incubation

"THRASHED OUT"

THEORETICALLY, PRACTICALLY,

AND

HISTORICALLY,

BY

C. CASHMORE,

LOUGHBOROUGH.

ONE SHILLING.

Loughborough:

PRINTED BY ALFRED CLARKE, 32, SWAN STREET.

1891.

INTRODUCTION.

Artificial Incubation having been before the public so many years it will be unnecessary for me to enlarge upon the possibility of incubating eggs artificially. That chicks, ducklings, etc., have been brought into existence by artificial means, without any assistance from the hen (after she has produced the eggs), and at times good results have been obtained by Incubators of the present day no one can deny. On the other hand, every one who has worked Incubators for any considerable time must admit that "some link in the chain" is missing—something hidden which has not been revealed—some error which occasionally causes great mortality, even to the loss of whole hatches. My aim therefore will be to unearth the monster, and to expose false theories.

Mr. Lewis Wright, in his Poultry Book, published some 15 or 20 years ago, referring to the Egyptians and their egg-ovens, says:—" We can well believe that there *are* secrets which they have only themselves extracted from nature by long study and observation, and these means alone will induce her to reveal them to us."

Since Mr. W. penned those lines, many new Incubators have been introduced to the public, and these secrets have been searched for continuously, but very few experimentalists have dived below the surface, *they* expected a temperature regulator to accomplish everything, and as it failed to do so, Artificial Incubation was given up by a large majority of them as hopeless. I do not know of any

Incubator having been placed on the market which has been nearer to the solution of the problem than that invented by Mr. Boyle 20 years ago, and I imagine that he abandoned his machine with its most sensitive regulator because he failed to discover these secrets, and had I not succeeded in capturing the monster during such a grand opportunity as presented itself by the continnation of unfavourable weather during the season 1891, I certainly should have followed Mr. Boyle into retirement; an Incubator which can only be depended upon when the weather is favourable can only be looked upon as a mere toy.

I must here ask the indulgence of my readers who have used my original Incubator; I very much regret that I failed to make my machine perfect at first. Josh Billings says: "We sumtimes hit a thing right the fust blow, but most always a suckcess iz the result ov menny failures." Well, I think my customers will admit that I came as near "hitting" as anyone; that I, with others, tripped over the same stumbling blocks. Where I failed others failed also. All that has been accomplished by any other Incubator has been accomplished by this one; given good eggs, favourable atmospheric influences and careful management it was quite possible to obtain the coveted 100 %, and this has been obtained by several of my customers.

I have been censured because I did not keep my invention more prominently before the public, but I knew there was something to discover, and preferred to concentrate my attention on research, rather than on a large output.

The Temperature Question.

We are informed by nearly all writers upon Artificial Incubation, that eggs must be maintained at 103 degs. Fahr. Several manufacturers of Incubators claim that they have produced a regulator, which, being placed in the nest, will maintain this temperature unaffected by external changes; but they make a proviso that two or three degs. variation either way is of no consequence, and a sudden rise of the barometer, they tell us, will not affect the regulators more than two or three degs.

It has been a mystery to me that I could not regulate my Incubator with a thermostat placed in the nest, while other makers do (so they say). The first regulating machine I made was fitted with a very sensitive thermostat which forced the flame of the lamp to a very small jet when the temperature was over 103, and enlarged the flame to full size when the temperature was under 103, but, owing to the time needed to cool and re-heat the water in the tank the temperature was constantly rising or falling between 100 and 106. I hatched chicks in this machine, and a report of the experiment was published in the *Live Stock Journal* early in the year 1879, but during a subsequent trial a rising barometer "cooked" the eggs and an accident directed me to the regulation of the temperature by the expansion and contraction of the water in the cistern, by which system I loyally stand.

Now any Engineer or Scientist who will "thrash out" the subject could tell us that metallic regulators, of themselves, are neither sensitive, nor quick enough for our purpose, and that air or spirits as the motive power are unreliable, owing to the influence the pressure of the

atmosphere exerts over them, and that no regulator, however sensitive, can maintain a perfectly even temperature
when placed in the nest of a hot water Incubator; but
presuming for the moment that all these difficulties have
been overcome, and that we can perfectly maintain 103
degs. Fahr. in the empty nest of an Incubator, would
this thermostat be correct? No! I do not wish to
be misunderstood upon this question. I do not assert that
eggs cannot be hatched by these regulators, my own
experience teaches me that some eggs will hatch almost
anyhow, but my study has been to produce an Incubator
which shall be able at all times and under all conditions
to hatch equal to the best sitting hen, and I assert a
regulator placed in the nest is false, unnatural, and
unscientific; it may look clear and smooth on the surface,
but we will get below; we will perform an experiment in
which all may join who have access to an Incubator of any
make and prove this assertion.

Provide three thermometers, all registering correctly,
fix them in various parts of the drawer of an Incubator
with the top of the bulb level with the top of the eggs,
surround one of these thermometers with eggs due to
hatch in a day or two, another with unfertile or dead eggs,
and the third with eggs in any other stage; now close the
drawer and at the next visit note the register given by all
three thermometers. Do they all indicate the same temperature? No! Is it possible to make them all indicate
the same temperature? No! not until all eggs have been
killed and thus reduced to the same condition.

The general reader and the scientist may now answer
the question, Is the temperature problem solved by a

regulator in the nest, or is the claim of some manu-facturers simply "business puff"?

Now it will be found on examining the thermometers that eggs nearly due to hatch are several degs. higher in temperature than 103, and that clear or dead eggs are much lower; here then is a source of great danger, expecially in the hands of a novice (not only with thermostatic Incubators, but with my original machine). If all eggs are fertile and strong, and the weather is favour-able, we may bring off good hatches with the temperature of the nest maintained at 103 degs. Fahr., but from the first to the last there is a "tug of war" between the life in the egg and the regulator; if the eggs hatch they have won; if they die in the shell they have lost, and that is all we have known about it, but if a large proportion of the eggs are weakly, and die during the second week, the mischief begins; at one time we have live eggs in close proximity to the thermometer, and we imagine the temperature is too high, and adjust the regulator accordingly; if now we move the eggs and bring dead ones in close proximity to the thermometer, the next time we visit the machine we find the temperature too low, and thus we are altering the setting of the temperature and perhaps killing those that otherwise would hatch.

I trust I have made it clear to my readers, that a thermostat or any other regulator placed in the nest is false, unnatural, and unscientific, and that even a thermometer in the nest is unreliable; we will now try if we cannot obtain something worthy of the name of regulator, and which will prove that even the problem of producing a temperature regulator has not before been solved; but before doing so it will be necessary to clear the ground somewhat.

Mr. Hearson says:—*" We made several forms of Incubators with tanks in which the water was regulated with such precision that it did not vary half a deg. day nor night for a week; but we found that a thermometer placed in the egg drawer varied fully half as much as the external air."

I do not know whether this experiment was made with a view to advance artificial incubation or to run down other systems. I can only meet the remark by a counter statement, that I can make a machine (I will not say Incubator) and fit it with a thermostatic regulator, and eggs placed in it shall vary quite as much as the external air; does this prove anything?

My most perfect Incubator (No. 4) has a tank of water surrounding the eggs—heat is applied below—by a natural law the water at the top of the tank is hotter than that at the bottom. The temperature is ascertained by a thermometer, which is immersed in the tank, and the water is automatically maintained at 104 degs. Fahr.; we have thus an artificial broody hen, always one temperature, always ready and willing to sit, eggs may be placed in the nest at any time and they regulate their own temperature exactly the same as they would do under a hen, and now a thermometer in the nest becomes useless, except as a scientific instrument which will tell us the correct temperature of eggs in various stages. During the first

* Artificial Incubation by C. E. Hearson. P. 19.

stage they are several degs. lower than the water in the tank, and at the hatching time higher.

I believe the evils caused by a regulator in the nest would never have been discovered but for this machine, which shows it in its true colours. Should we raise the temperature of the water in the tank two degs., the thermometer in the drawer with the eggs will not rise half a deg., and should we lower the temperature of the water in the tank two degs., the thermometer in the drawer with the eggs will not fall half a deg., and should we reduce the temperature of eggs due to hatch to 100 degs. Fahr., it would be necessary to reduce the heat of the water in the tank to 90, therefore instead of the eggs varying half as much as the external atmosphere, they do not vary half as much as the water in the tank (except the increase of heat as life advances), and the water being automatically maintained at an uniform temperature, we need no diagram to shew the variations upon the eggs; whereas with a so-called regulator in the nest, regulation is impossible.

The question may now be asked, is it not an evil applying heat below the eggs? Mr. Hearson says:*"Any apparatus which heats the eggs from below I have no hesitation in pronouncing a failure without further examination, as out of 800 eggs experimented upon in several Incubators supplying heat from below I only succeeded in hatching two chickens."

This shows to what an extent anyone is liable to be deceived when making experimental research, and the material of which our "theory" is built. All writers during the last 20 years, whom I have consulted, condemn

* Artificial Incubation by C. E. Hearson. P. 41.

applying heat below the eggs; some inform us that
they require to be kept warm on the upper and cold on
the lower side. but none of them *know*. Such writers as
Mr. Lewis Wright and Mr. Edward Brown are careful not
to commit themselves by assertions they cannot prove, but
the amount of trash that has been published in pamphlets
and poultry papers by experimentalists generally is
surprising; some perform an experiment—it comes off
satisfactorily, they rush into print with the solution of the
problem; perhaps before the ink is dry a repetition of the
same experiment is a complete failure. Some perform an
experiment which turns out a failure, and the thing is
condemned without further examination, when perhaps
they have put the "shoe ou the wrong foot;" and other
experimentalists are held back by these assertions. I have
not selected this assertion of Mr. Hearson's because it held
me back, as I did not see his work until I had succeeded
where he had failed. The very thing which he so strongly
condemns has proved a stepping stone to me. I care
nothing now for all the theories and assertions put forth
by experimentalists; I have stepped out of the old rut
some time ago, and "set up" for myself.

Well now, we have the temperature settled—we apply
heat below—keep the "old hen" always at one temperature,
unaffected by thermal or barometrical influences, surely
the problem is solved? No; it has not been, and never
will be, solved by a temperature question alone. We may
keep the temperature perfect, and fail miserably, owing to
some error elsewhere, but we have settled the regulation
difficulty, and will search elsewhere for the missing link.

The Moisture Question.

The theory held by all interested in the science of artificial incubation, is, that eggs require to be kept in a moist atmosphere, and that water for the purpose of creating vapour in Incubators is an absolute necessity. Messrs. Boyle, Penman, Voitellier, Christy, Howell, Tomlinson, Hearson, Hillier, Field, Lathbury, and other experimentalists, have appliances of some description for creating vapour in their Incubators. For upwards of 15 years I have been a follower of this theory, and with Mr. Edward Brown, was of opinion "that it is impossible to give too much moisture by evaporation."

The greatest known enemy we have had to fear has been a dry E. wind, and during the prevalence of these winds it has not been possible to give *enough* moisture by evaporation, and at times eggs are dried up, even if they are sprinkled two or three times a day.

There has also been another enemy which has been overlooked or unnamed *i.e.* a saturated atmosphere. We may pass through several seasons, and only receive a transient visit, but during the season 1891 it was almost a constant attendant.

Mr. Cook, in *Poultry*, of March 20th, 1891, says :— " So far this season I find there are very few chickens about ; I have not heard of any very good results from hens, but still less from Incubators, so many chickens having died in the shell. I use one of H ——'s, and the mysterious thing about it is, that although it does not vary 2° in six weeks, the chickens die in the shells, not for the want of moisture, as that I take particular notice of."

Mr. Cook is quite correct, it was not for want of moisture. If he will make enquiries at the Meteorological Station of his district he will probably find that the atmosphere during his trial, was thoroughly saturated.

An experimentalist, some years ago, attributed the losses during such weather to miasma; and prescribed fresh lime in the drawer as a remedy. Some have suggested Condy's Fluid. Some have tried greasing the eggs, and some have even gone so far as to try smoke drying them, by burning a paraffin lamp directly under the nest. but still the secret which Mr. Lewis Wright spoke of nearly 20 years ago is undiscovered and a moisture theory is reigning supreme.

Mr. Hearson says:*" those who are acquainted with Dalton's tables of the tension of water vapour, will know that the amount of aqueous vapour which the air will carry with it depends on the temperature, and as this is constant, the moisture will always be the same." I would suggest to Mr. H. the advisibility of looking up Dalton again before he repeats this assertion, as anyone who carefully reads the laws referred to will know that this law is not applicable to Incubators, the amount of vapour the air *will* carry, and the amount it *does* carry, when subject to atmospheric influences, are two different things. No system of moistening the air in Incubators by the application of moisture trays can create an uniform humidity ; unless the humidity amounts to complete saturation, and complete saturation is tantamount to complete failure, If Dalton's laws are applicable to Incubators, where would the difficulty arise in keeping a

* Artificial Incubation, by C. E. Hearson. P. 20.

moist atmosphere in a "sick" room? Simply placing pails of water in the room would accomplish the object, the temperature being constant the moisture *should* be the same.

I have performed experiments with moisture in every conceivable way, and results have been anything but satisfactory. In genial weather. with eggs from strong, well fed fowls, we may bring off good hatches, but during an exceptionally dry or damp atmosphere, failure more or less becomes the rule. In dry weather we cannot give enough moisture by evaporation, and in damp weather chicks are drowned in the shells if we give none. It is not an enviable occupation to sit by the side of an Incubator to remove moisture trays in damp weather, to replace them in genial, and to sprinkle the eggs when the atmosphere is dry. I could not see hens carrying moisture in dry and withholding it in damp weather; therefore I began to look upon our moisture theory with suspicion. We are told in support of this theory, that hens bring off better hatches when they "steal" their nest and make it in a hedge bottom, than they do when sitting in a poultry house.

Is this so? If a hen brings off a good hatch from a stolen nest, there is as a rule no secret made of the occurrence, it is something to talk about : but if she spoils all the eggs, nobody knows anything about it. I would suggest that when a hen brings off an unusually good hatch from a stolen nest it is because she laid all the eggs herself, whereas another hen sitting in the poultry house has been supplied with a mixed lot of eggs. We all know that eggs from some birds *will* hatch, while those from another will *not*, under the same conditions of incubation

Also, do not hens in exceptionally dry places hatch all the eggs sometimes?

Has anyone tried making a nest in a damp place? If so, I imagine they would soon find the hen "sitting standing."

Some will assert they sprinkle the nest when the eggs are due to hatch, with good results.

Can anyone prove they would not have hatched without this treatment?

Do hens naturally choose a damp place?

Everyone who has worked Incubators must vote the moisture question a nuisance, even if it were satisfactory and reliable, but Experimentalists, Manufacturers, and "the Press," all unite in asserting we cannot do without it; let us try, we are quite convinced that if there is a secret to be discovered, we *must* remove the moisture question before we shall be able to find it.

We have perfected the regulation of temperature, and can bring off better hatches during genial weather than we could twelve years ago, but during the extremes of atmospheric influences comparative failure still follows us; therefore we will abandon "moisture" and search elsewhere.

Ventilation.

All Incubators have some arrangements for the admission of fresh air to the eggs, and for the discharge of vitiated air.

Some experimentalists have tried regulating the temperature by a valve or damper, which retards the ventilation when the temperature is too low, and increases it when too high; but the system most generally adopted is to regulate the heat applied, and allow a constant and regular supply of fresh air (or rather, they tell us it is constant and regular; the atmospheric influences which cause more or less draught, are not taken into consideration). I do not see much alteration in the ventilation during the last fifteen years, but it is interesting and amusing to read the various claims put forth by manufacturers; some advertising in their prospectuses and the "Poultry" papers, "ours is the only scientific method," but when we come to examine it, we find it only an imitation of twenty years ago.

One manufacturer, however, steps boldly out and tells us, "six or eight times as much air as is necessary for the supply of all the chicken, which can be hatched in any particular sized Incubator, passes through the ventilating holes." Another surpasses this by "supplying about ten times more ventilation than would be possible in a hot water Incubator." I suppose my readers will expect me to beat the record by giving twenty times more than would be possible in a hot air Incubator, but I am not in this competition; I believe "enough is as good as a feast and too much of a good thing an evil."

Now, is the amount of air passing through any Incubator of the present day regular at all times ? Anyone who has the management of a stove, or ordinary fire grate, can answer this question in the negative. During a dry atmosphere, with a high barometer, the rush of air through an Incubator or stove is considerable, but when the atmosphere is saturated, and the barometer low, there is scarcely any ventilation through an Incubator; and I have known the current to enter at the top and escape at the bottom. Here then, we have the two extremes of atmospheric influences which have been fatal to artificial incubation. The first is known as E. wind, and is really a dry and heavy atmosphere, the rush of air through Incubators at this time carries the moisture from the tray, and from the eggs with it, and we complain of insufficiency of moisture. The other has never been named, it is generally set down as E. wind, but it is a damp and light atmosphere ; at this time there is scarcely any air passing through an Incubator and fires can scarcely be made to burn.

The latter evil was the chief cause of poor results obtained by Incubators and hens generally during the season, 1891. It will now be understood why success and failure have been obtained by the same Incubator, and under the same management.

We are told, that we have perfect regulators, scientific moistening and ventilating arrangements, yet only in genial weather can we bring off good hatches ; but if the weather is unfavourable, and the question is asked, Why have I failed ? The reply is "we do not know," or "atmospheric influences." Sometime ago I read in a newspaper, that a great American Electrical Inventor stated in a law court, that he knew nothing about theory, and did not wish to know ; had he studied theory he would have been prevented from making experiments. I am of opinion that I should have perfected my Incubator years ago, *but* for "theory."

Theory says, we *must* apply top heat only ; we *must* ascertain the temperature by a thermometer in the nest. We *must* have moisture. Remove any one of these legs and down comes the tripod.

This is so, and like a three-legged stool, it sometimes comes to grief without removing a leg ; but the difficulty is overcome by removing *all* the legs.

I apply heat below. I ascertain the temperature by a thermometer in the tank. I banish the moisture trays for something better and less troublesome.

I will not weary my readers by taking them through the various experiments which led to the discovery. The secret has been hidden all these years under the moisture theory, and when this was removed we had only to search under ventilation.

Truth is sometimes stranger than fiction, and is it not strange that after various *"only scientific methods"* of ventilation have been before the public for years, a patent-able method should remain to be discovered, which would revolutionise the whole theory of artificial incubation ?

The ventilation, according to my latest discovery (which is secured by provisional protection), is now so arranged that the superfluous damp in the atmosphere cannot enter the nest, also the E. wind has now no power to rob the eggs of their natural moisture.

After upwards of fifteen years research, I have discovered that eggs are made perfect, and are supplied by nature with sufficient moisture for hatching purposes. I am rather ashamed to make this statement, and I throw all the blame on "theory," but by way of excuse I would remind my readers that unfavourable weather was the only favourable opportunity for making research in artificial incubation; however, I was prepared for the opportunity when presented, and a perfect, natural, and scientific method of ventilation, which has effectually removed the vexatious moisture theory, is the result.

How do I prove the moisture theory false? By the same means that I use to prove the temperature theory false. By the Incubator itself, thus:—

Start two Incubators, try one without moisture, and the other with ; in the one the eggs are dry until hatching time, then, when they "chip" the moisture supplied by nature escapes from the fracture made by the chicks —creates a natural moist atmosphere in the nest, and they hatch out healthy ; but in the other, a large proportion of the chicks will be drowned in the shell, exactly the same as they were in a large number of Incubators during the saturated atmosphere of the past season, and I challenge anyone to contradict my assertion, "that eggs are supplied by nature with sufficient moisture for hatching purposes."

The answer to the questions—Why are so many chicks dead in the shells? Why have so many deformed feet? can now be found in the moisture theory.

I stand alone at present as an opposer of this theory, but the time will soon come when any Incubator having any connecton with this theory will be looked upon with suspicion.

Mr. Edward Browu says:—"Certaioly Incubators are useful, but they require brains to work them." It will now be plaiu to everyone where the "braius" have been needed.

We have all been under the iufluence of '*Hydrocephalus*' and have been fighting against natural laws, aud now we wonder that we could produce chicks at all with our unnatural treatment.

THEN, we did not know the correct temperature for eggs under incubation. Now, we do.

THEN, we were misled by a thermometer iu the nest. Now, we are not.

THEN, we were liable to accident by a rising barometer. Now, we are not.

THEN, we were liable to drown the chicks iu the shell. Now, we are not.

THEN, we were liable to dry them up, Now, we are not.

THEN, we were groping in the dark, almost bewildered during unfavourable weather by the mauagemeut of an Incubator. Now, darkness gives place to light, and artificial incubation becomes one of the simplest things in the world.

Nearly all great inventions have been perfected by the removal of complications, and it is just so with artificial incubation. We began wrong; we tried adding other wrongs to make a right, and consequently we required "brains" to work the machines.

All complications of regulators and calculations as to temperature are removed. We bow to nature, filter the atmosphere, remove the moisture trays, and at last we have an Incubator, which at all seasons will surpass hens, if they are not on their best behaviour.

CASHMORE'S
AUTOMATIC + INCUBATOR.

THE PIONEER.

FIRST INTRODUCED IN 1879.

Historical.

The Incubator, as illustrated on the preceding page, was invented by me and first introduced to the public in 1879, as an improvement upon the Hydro-Incubators, which at that time had gained some notoriety as the result of a Tournament held at Hemel Hempstead in 1878. In answer to announcements appearing in "the Press" that the trial would be repeated in 1879, I entered this machine. which gained second place. This competition is now matter for history, but for reasons best known to the Committee some facts were withheld. This history would certainly have been more interesting and perhaps more beneficial to the public had the Report been written by the " Disappointed Competitors."

Prof. Long, in his Poultry Book, says :—" Next came the Incubator invented and exhibited by Cashmore, which won second prize at the Hemel Hempstead Tournament, the temperature of the egg drawer during the twenty-one days' trial varying between 96° and 104°, fifty seven per cent. of the eggs being hatched." This is quite correct so far as it goes, and history goes no further. I suppose the inference drawn from this and similar statements would be that the machine was unmanageable, owing to the heat varying 9°, whereas a table of the official register with an explanation, would have shown this inference to be erroneous. The explanation, which should in all fairness have accompanied the report, is—on the morning of the 7th day the lamp in this Incubator was found to have been misplaced ; a statement made by the person in charge that " he found a cat in the room," was accepted by the Committee, but *did not appear in their Report.*

The following Table which is copied from "Artificial Incubation," by Mr. Edward Brown, will prove that during the earliest infancy of this machine the temperature *was* under control. At this early date I was of opinion that the temperature, as ascertained by a thermometer in the nest, should be lower during the early than during the latter stages of incubation.

No. 2 Cashmore's Lamp, hatched 57·14 %.

No. of Days ...	1	2	3	4	5	6	7	8	9	10	11	12
Heat in (Morn.	103½	100	100	99	100	100	96	101	102½	102	102	104
Drawer (Night	100	100	100	101	102	101	102½	100	104	102½	102	102½

No. of Days ...	13	14	15	16	17	18	19	20	21	22	23
Heat in (Morn.	102	102	102	102½	102	99	102	103	103	102	104
Drawer (Night	104½	103	105	104½	102	105	104	104	103	104	...

Had it been my duty or privilege to write the history of that competition I should have said a word or two with reference to the egg shells having been destroyed ; each lot of eggs was marked with a signature, and no two lots were endorsed by the same person ; this was, according to rule, to prevent fraud. As the chicks hatched out, they and the egg shells were removed by the person in charge. but, when the competition terminated, chicks only were presented to the judge, the shells when called for were not forthcoming, *they had been destroyed*. This fact, together with the discovery of another Hydro-Incubator on the premises, and other mysterious circumstances confirmed all the competitors, except the winner, into "disappointed competitors."

As one result of this competition Hydro-Incubators were the machines of the day. Another result was the creation of an impetus, which started inventors after a regulator.

Oh, for a Regulator! A kingdom for a Regulator!

This imaginary beacon was searched for with all the energy of enthusiasm, but many explorators soon discovered that they were following a "will o' the wisp," and retired muttering, "artificial incubation is a failure." Others cried " Eureka! " at first sight of the "ignis fatuus" careless of the mud and disappointment.

Away from Hemel Hempstead the "Hydro" Incubator was unable to maintain its standard at $97^0/_0$, and, strange to say, such was the force of the reaction in public opinion that after persuading the poultry world that lamps and regulators were answerable for previous failures, and that the cure for all diseases in artificial incubation could be found only in *Hydropathy*, the inventor of this "star of the first magnitude" actually adopted a lamp and regulator himself.

Metallic regulators, however, soon found a rival; a discovery was made that there is nothing like air, *so* sensitive, but when the barometer began to play with it, this was allowed to stand down.

Soon another thermostatic regulator appeared upon the stage—a "Spirit" Regulator. Although its inventor strongly denounced "supplying heat from below," he did not say that this regulator was supplied from above. But, being infallable, could this have been the production of any ordinary mortal? Its introducer claimed that it had "solved the problem of how to maintain a regular temperature *within* 5°." Did not admit failure to be possible. Said it was "the *only* thermostatic incubator in the world." Pointed at *others* as "worthless imitations," and assumed for it a title. This was not all; through the Press he said :— "Mine is the best Incubator in the world, but no other maker will give me an opportunity of testing my machine by the side of theirs." The opportunity was immediately offered, but the offer, although acknowledged, was not accepted.

Query—Do the laws of the arena allow a gladiator, who will not fight, to assume the title of " Champion? "

The Automatic Incubator, which fought in the battle of Hemel Hempstead, which won a second rate position, and divided the lines of the Boillng Water Forces, was, and is, open to another engagement under amended rules. It never claimed "perfection" for one of its names, but it did, and does claim Equality.

We next had a new departure, in the form of " Atmospheric Incubators." These were the production of experimentalists who were dissatisfied with the results they obtained when using thermostatic hot water machines. I have been favoured with opportunities of overhauling some of these Incubators, and I consider that if the problem is to be solved by a perfectly regular temperature, as ascertained by a thermometer in the nest, this was a step in the right direction; but if the solution depends upon more closely following nature these machines must soon "stand down." I cannot imagine anything more outrageous than placing eggs in a riddle, and allowing a paraffin lamp to play amongst them.

Time and space forbid the mention of all the actors in this drama, but as very few are endowed with sufficient *nerve* for "stars" I trust they will overlook the omission.

We can now survey the course right back to Hemel Hempstead ; here we behold the whole exploring army searching for something—following an *ignis fatuus*, and tramping through the mud, " Regulator in the Nest," and " Moisture " blazoned on their banners.

Oh, yes! I was drawn into the current, but I have landed high and dry ; have planted a danger signal "Beware of Moisture," and unfurled

A banner with the strange device—" Excelsior! "

During the exploration of this dark continent of Artificial Incubation two burning questions were before the country, one—Why are so many chicks dead in the shell? Very few attempts were made to answer this question. The " Champion " said "we do not know," but he promised a reward to any who would communicate the answer. Here it is—because the eggs have been treated unnaturally. The other—Why have so many chicks deformed feet? An elaborate answer to this question was attempted by the " Scientist " to the effect that it was caused by noise, such as hammering, passing trains, vibration of floors, &c. Do not believe such rubbish ! Deformed feet are the result of cramp engendered before, or during hatching by "moisture."

Moral—Do not place too great faith in advertisements, or you may find, when too late, that "all is not gold that glitters."

Practical.

Having cleared the ground somewhat and described the development of the Incubator, we will now endeavour to describe the management.

As before stated the temperature is automatically regulated by the expansion and contraction of the water in the tank :—A float or piston which rides on the water, is connected, as illustrated on the following page, to the burner of a nicely balanced lamp ; the result being that if the heat of the water rises the flame of the lamp is reduced and vice-versâ. This action being immediate the variations are almost nil, because a rise of one degree would ,reduce the flame of the lamp from the largest to the smallest possible size.

To make this quite clear, and to illustrate how to solve a problem : Imagine a large thermometer, apply a moveable lamp to the bulb, let a piston ride on the mercury in the tube and connect it, by beam and rods, to the lamp. If necessary arrangements have been made, it will now automatically regulate the temperature and the thermometer is converted into a thermostat; now make an insertion in the bulb, place eggs therein, and the thermostat becomes a *Thermostatic Incubator*, i.e. an Incubator being a self-acting apparatus for regulating temperature.

Now we are ready to unpack the machine and commence operations.

Fix it in any convenient room which is well ventilated. Fill the tank with rain water, heated to 106 degs. Fahr. Fill and light the lamp, join the connections, and allow the temperature to settle.

CASHMORE'S
PATENT
AUTOMATIC ✛ INCUBATOR,
No. 4.

THE MASTERPIECE.

THE KEY WHICH UNLOCKED THE MYSTERY.

After the machine has been running for an hour or two note the register of the tank thermometer, if it is registering above the "red mark" put a little water into the tank: if below, draw off a little at the tap. A small measure is supplied which holds sufficient water to alter the temperature one deg.

When the temperature *of the water in the tank* is settled at 104 degs. Fahr., place in the drawer the eggs on which the date should be written.

Turn the eggs twice daily and allow them to cool somewhat.

Fill the lamp daily; if benzoline is used it will only require trimming once or twice during the season; if paraffin is used it will need trimming more frequently.

Examine the eggs on the 5th day, by holding them before a small light in a dark room, and remove unfertile ones ; these may be used for cooking purposes, or be saved for the chicks.

On the 20th day look carefully for "chips," and turn the chipped side uppermost.

Duck and Bantum eggs may be put in the drawer at the same time, if desirable.

Owing to variations, in different localities, of the price of benzoline and paraffin, I do not quote cost, but give the quantity required for each machine. I also give the area of each drawer.

Number of Eggs.	Size of Drawer.	Quantity of Benzoline or Paraffin consumed.
30	11-ins. by 12-ins.	3 quarts in 4 weeks.
60	15 .. 16 ,,	4 ., 4 ,,
120	21 .. 24 ,,	6 ,, 4 ,,

This Table was compiled when the thermometer in the room was registering from 50° to 60°. More oil will be consumed if the room is colder, and less if warmer. Also about double the quantity will be used during the first than during the last week of incubation; the chicks during the last week supply heat naturally, therefore they do not require to be supplied with so much artificially.

Please compare cost aud tronble of working this machine with that of any other.

NOTICE.

Manufacturers please note, that according to "Nuttall" the name "Thermostatic Incubator" belongs only to Cashmore's Machine. Anyone using it after this notice will be dubbed usurpers. They may use the words Thermostat with an Incubator, Incubator with a Thermostat, Will with a Wisp, or any other synonym, but Thermostatic Incubator is not theirs by right. See Page 26.

CASHMORE'S

PATENT

AUTOMATIC ✢ INCUBATOR,

No. 2.

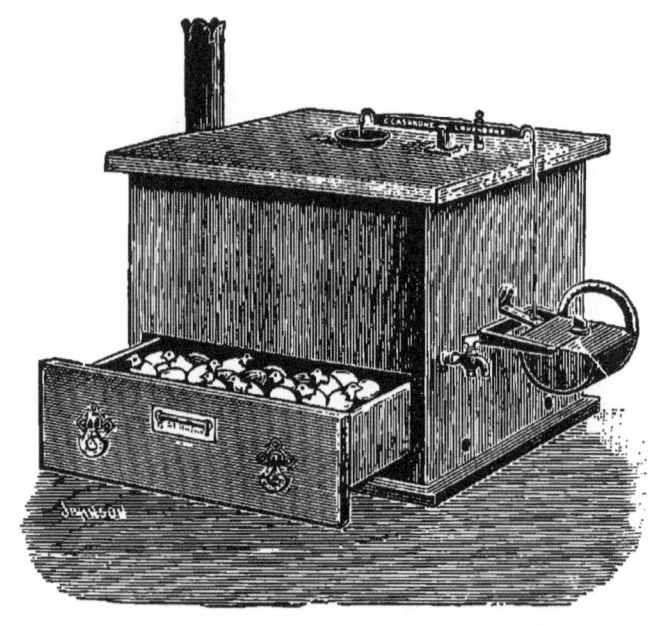

THE OLD FRIEND WITH A NEW FACE.

An Old Friend with a New Face.

Having unearthed the monsters and out of chaos produced an Incubator, we can now take our Old Friend in hand and use the knowledge obtained from the "Pullet" to teach the "Old Hen" how to hatch eggs.

First we observe the machine has been suffering from the effects of "dropsy," therefore we clear out the moisture trays with all their accumulation of mould and germ, and this disease "dries up." Now do not run away with the idea that this was the only machine affected ; no the disease *was* common to all.

Its next fault was, its inability to radiate so much heat to the lower side of the eggs in cold as in warm weather. Now do not imagine that *this* complaint affected this machine and did *not* affect others. We have been informed that a thermostat placed in the nest will maintain a regular temperature unaffected by external variations, but the thermometer, to prove this assertion, is never placed on the bottom of the nest or drawer ; it is only put there to run down the other fellow. Now this disease is common to all "top heat" strain ; the only remedy we can offer is—to keep it in a warm room ; this disease, however, is "bred out" in our new "strain."

Another fault was, its inability to *keep eggs* always at one temperature, *others* had solved the problem of how to accomplish this impossibility, but *we* had not. This bubble has been exposed in a previous chapter.

We have been informed that in this machine (or this system) the temperature upon the eggs varies half as much as the external air, and that a tank of water kept at one temperature cannot keep the heat of a drawer placed below it at anything like a regular temperature; these assertions are false. We are willing to admit all our faults, but will not carry exaggerated burdens. We admit it is affected by external variations to the extent of $10^o/_o$; now if 5° variation is allowed in other Incubators, it will need a rise in the external temperature of 50° before the margin is exceeded in this one. We do know when to expect a rise or fall in the external atmosphere, and can generally meet it half way, but when the barometer plays with air and spirit regulators it does so when least expected, and can *not* be guarded against. We claim that this machine will keep *something like* a regular temperature, and is unaffected by barometrical influences.

Although this machine cannot approach our No. 4, either in simplicity, results obtainable, or quality of produce, it is in advance of any other make, and we are prepared to prove our assertion by competitive trials.

CASHMORE'S

PATENT

AUTOMATIC INCUBATOR,
No. 5.

THE ACCOMMODATION.

To Burn Gas.

This Incubator has been specially designed to meet the requirements of those persons who have access to gas, and prefer this system of heating. An ordinary paraffin lamp is fitted to the machine, for use when the gas is cut off, or in case of emergency.

The expansion of the water in the tank opens a valve which allows the superfluous heat to escape.

Like our No. 4 Incubator, the water in the tank is maintained at 104 degs. Fahr., but the quantity of oil consumed in this stationary lamp is double that consumed in our moveable one.

Proposition—If one gal. of oil is required to work this Incubator for two weeks, where the water in the tank is maintained at 104 degs. Fahr., how much will be required to maintain the temperature in thermostat-in-the-incubator machines at 125 to 135 degs. for the same period.

Well now, the search in artificial incubation is ended, and my task is done ; I have endeavoured, in a plain way, to expose errors, to unearth the monster, and to refute misstatements. It has been necessary during the "thrashing out" to use the flail rather heavily at times, but necessity demanded it, and I regret the necessity.

At the time of writing these chapters I have no testimonials to offer, except those referring to past history. I therefore ask my readers, before giving their verdict, to consult the other side, and if they decide for them and the old theories, they should by all means stand to their old guns, but if they decide to throw in their lot with the "revolution" I shall be pleased to receive their commands, which shall have my careful attention. If, however, they are undecided, my advice is—watch the battle, and await the result.

Rearing.

We now come to another very interesting subject, viz.: rearing the chicks ; the three weeks of "watching and waiting" are ended, and the anxiously expected little visitors have arrived; the question now naturally arises, can we rear them without the assistance of hens? and if so, can it be accomplished economically?

If eggs are put into the Incubator as they are laid, and hens can be set at the same time, it is good policy to give the chicks to the hens, a hen can generally brood more than she can hatch, and 10 or 12 chicks are rather troublesome rearing artificially : but if we can procure 30 or more, (the more the better) at one time, they certainly can be reared without the hen, and at less cost and trouble than with.

In genial weather there is no difficulty whatever, but as with incubation so with rearing, we have to provide against ungenial atmospheric influences.

The greatest enemy we have to fear is "cramp," which is exaggerated, if not engendered, by a cold, saturated atmosphere. There is very little difficulty in rearing chicks either artificially, or naturally, during frosty weather, but when the atmosphere is saturated, and the thermometer about 40 degs., with a low barometer, and cold winds, hens cannot successfully rear chicks without assistance, and it is the most trying time for rearing them artificially, however with suitable houses we can overcome the difficulty, and rear them successfully.

Rearers in general use are tanks of hot water, which radiate heat upon chicks. After using this class of brooder for many years, I have abandoned it for something better. The same natural law which in winter prevents heat descending sufficiently in Incubators, prevents this system being adopted in rearers with anything approaching success, as the backs of the chicks are too hot, while their feet and legs are benumbed This treatment often amounts to cruelty.

Most writers upon the subject of rearing, condemn the use of greenhouses, but, in no instance have I heard of any attempt to overcome the difficulty, they say "the chicks will die of cramp if placed therein." but the "why" is not entered into by any of them. *They* have tried and failed, so it is useless anyone trying again.

I should not be surprised to learn that the first attempt to grow flowers and fruit in a greenhouse was a failure, and that the present efficiency of "glass" is due to experimental research. What has been done in the way of attempts at rearing chicks, &c. under glass? All the information I can gain upon the subject is something like this. Someone had a hen with a few chicks, say in January, and as the weather was unfavourably cold, he, thinking to benefit them, placed them in a greenhouse, where very soon cramp made its appearance. Now we know something respecting cramp; it is a complaint which affects the legs and is somewhat akin to rheumatism, we also know that a cold damp atmosphere is favourable to the development of this complaint and if we are to guard against it we must keep their legs warm and dry, without roasting their backs; let anyone, before he places chickens in a greenhouse, take off his shoes and have a turn for an hour or two himself, well, I think the imagination will be sufficient to give cramp. Now is this treatment likely to succeed? Flowers are growing in the greenhouse; they thrive, why should we fail with chicks? It is just this, we give the flowers a suitable place on the stage, and we put the chickens under. If we réverse the usual order for once, put the chicks on the stage and the flowers under, I know the chicks will thrive, and I imagine the flowers will have the cramp.

The same thing occurs if we use a Rearer in the greenhouse, and place it under the stage, neither hen nor Rearer can compete against the cold damp floor under the stage.

Well we have hatched the chicks, what must we do with them? and how can we do without a Brooder radiating heat upon their backs? By using my new Brooder, which has no lamp, and therefore no heat to radiate. I quite expect it will take me some time to convince the public that chicks can be reared in these Brooders, and therefore I propose to supply old pattern Brooders for the convenience of those who are sceptical, but I can assert, there is no difficulty whatever; after the chicks are thoroughly dry (say in 24 hours), if 30 are put in one of these Brooders and are shut in, they will be perfectly contented and happy, their own animal heat is quite sufficient to keep them warm.

In genial weather they may be kept in any snug room or poultry house, but some arrangements must be made for warming the room, or, removing them to a warmer one during inclement weather; it is now not a question of heating the Brooder, but the room they are reared in. When using the old pattern Brooders the errors of incubation followed us in rearing, and we again used two wrongs to make a right, but now we warm the room if the weather is unfavourable, and the chicks provide their own fuel when nestling in the Brooder.

My system is this, I use an ordinary greenhouse, the stages are covered with slates or boards; under the stages are circulating pipes, which in severe weather are kept warm by a slow-combustion stove, the stages are covered with garden soil (which should be changed periodically), and on this are placed the Brooder and chicks; if the temperature is about 50 degs., Fahr. and the atmosphere genial, the chicks need no assistance from the stove. When they are tired of eating and running about, they retire to their nest and keep each other warm; no fear now of roasting them. But I imagine my sceptical reader will say, are you not afraid of a sudden fall of temperature killing them, if it comes on in the night? No! I have no fear on that account; they are comfortably housed for the night, and will come through all right, but in the day time we warm the place if they show signs of needing it. If we keep the room very cold they will stay in the Brooder for warmth, but if we encourage them with a little fire they will soon be out and scratching for the little dainty morsels we bury in the soil for them, and will repay our extra trouble by growing more quickly. What about cramp? Well, since I adopted this plan two years ago, I have seen no symptoms of cramp in the greenhouse, but have placed chicks therein which were taken from a hen, undoubtedly suffering from the disease, and they soon recovered.

On the top of the stages divisions may be made, and the front should have wire mesh placed round it to keep the chicks from getting off. The greenhouses should also have windows which can be opened in warm weather for ventilation, and the openings should be covered with wire mesh to keep chicks in and cats out.

The spaces underneath the stage can be utilized by the chicks when they are old enough to discard the Brooder, and in that case openings should be made in the walls, and pens attached for the chicks to run in and out, but it would be advisable not to use this space unless the weather is favourable.

Those who are not in possession of a spare greenhouse may soon convert any spare room into a suitable rearing house. All they have to do is to rig up a table or stage for the chicks, and warm the room when needed) by a stove or ordinary fire grate. have a window, if possible on the sunny side, which can be opened in warm weather for ventilation. and when the weather is favourable the Brooder and chicks may be transferred to a chicken pen or poultry house, or may simply be surrounded with wire mesh, and be moved about as desired.

The illustration on page 48 shows the section of a movable Rearing-house as supplied by me. It is constructed to hold one or two lots of chickens in the upper division, and one lot in the lower one; a pen should be attached to the lower appartment for the use of the chicks. The upper appartment is warmed by an ordinary paraffin lamp. It will be now observed that hot brooders are a useless encumbrance; in warm weather we may rear chicks with them, but the hot tank is then unnecessary, and liable to cause injury to the chicks. We require a warm room to

use my new Brooder in, and so we do with the old ones.
If by an accident the lamp goes out when using a hot
Brooder, it generally happens that a large number of the
chicks are found dead next morning. This is owing to the
cold water in the tank robbing the chicks of their warmth,
whereas with my new Brooders the animal heat generated
by the chicks is conserved and retained in the machine to
the advantage of the chicks and our pockets, and now all
we have to do is to see the chicks are well fed, look after
the ventilation and cleaning of the rearing houses, and
supply a little warmth when necessary.

A FEW OF THE MANY

TESTIMONIALS

RECEIVED REFERRING TO

CASHMORE'S ORIGINAL INCUBATOR.

"I am pleased to inform you that I have been very successful with your Lamp Incubator, having hatched 88 ducks from 113 eggs during the season, and in the last drawer full which was hatched in June, I had 89 chicks out of 42 eggs. I have never had such good results when setting under hens."—*John Clarke, Woodbrooke Cottage, Loughborough.*

"The Incubator is a complete success, every egg as yet has hatched true to the day, fine strong chicks. I am delighted with it."—*Austin Biggs, St. Peter's Schools, Bromyard, October 8, 1879.*

"Some time ago I bought an Incubator from Mr. Cashmore of Loughborough. The description of the machine given in the FANCIERS' CHRONICLE induced me to try it. I had no experience in the working of an Incubator, never having seen one of any sort before. I placed seven eggs in the drawer on July 3rd, and on the 23rd had five chicks hatched. On the 24th I put in some fresh eggs, and again on the 25th, 26th, and

28th, in all 43 eggs. Out of these 38 hatched, 3 had dead chicks in, and 2 were addled. I should add that mine is one of the Lamp Incubators, and I found it very easy to manage."--*Miss E. B., from* FANCIERS' CHRONICLE, *Nov. 14, 1875.*

" I have been using one of Cashmore's Lamp Incubators this season and am quite satisfied with it, and am fully persuaded that for amateurs it is the best machine. My first hatch of 11 eggs all hatched.--" *Gerard H. Fitzherbert, from* LIVE STOCK JOURNAL, *June 4, 1880.*

" I find the lamp very simple and to require far less attention than any other I have tried."--*O. Ernest Cresswell, Esq., Morney Cross, near Hereford, Sept. 1880.*

" I am glad to inform you that the Incubator I purchased from you some time ago has proved in every way quite a success, and this being my first attempt at Artificial Incubation, the results (which I give below) have quite surpassed my anticipation.

" 1st hatch, out of 22 hen eggs, 18 proved fertile, and 15 hatched out fine strong chicks.

" 2nd hatch, 31 ducks' eggs, 21 proved fertile, 18 hatched out ; also 11 hen eggs, of which 10 were fertile, 8 hatched out."--*Thos. Pattison, Aislaby, Pickering, Yorkshire, Sept. 7, 1880.*

" Since writing you last I have had another hatch of chickens, this time with even greater success than before. Out of 33 fertile eggs I got 32 chickens, equal to a percentage of 96·96, a result which I am sure speaks volumes for your machine."--*Thos. Pattison.*

" I have now given the 50 egg Incubator I had of you a second trial, with great success, having hatched 23 strong chickens from 30 eggs, the other seven I removed at the expiration of seven days, so that not one was lost. I am so pleased with it that I shall not trust valuable eggs with hens in the future. The simplicity of your machine is its recommendation ; it requires so little attendance. I have worked it without varying more than two degrees night or day."--*F. Shepherd, Poultry Cottage, Hathern Station, Jan. 18, 1882.*

" I was surprised to find in your issue of the 20th that Cashmore's Incubators are not mentioned. Anything more simple, more perfect, and less likely to get out of order I cannot imagine. I bought an old one almost by accident a long time since, have used it with great success for three seasons, and thoroughly believe that every fertile and fresh egg, even to a fortnight old, will be sure to hatch out.

I don't know Mr. Cashmore. I have no interest in selling the machine, but am simply an aged clergyman no longer equal to work, and amuse myself, while waiting, in hatching and rearing chickens, finding one of the above Lamp Incubators an agreeable companion even in my bedroom.

Further information will with pleasure be given as soon as permitted. Having the above machine I would not risk any valuable egg under any hen, and only wish you or anyone with influence would try one, so that they may be generally known for the general good. — *Yours sincerely*, *P. Parker Smith, 21, St. James' Place, Plymouth, April 24th.*

P.S. — The Lamp requires trimming only once a season, quarter pint of benzoline added every twenty-four hours, the eggs turned and aired once a day, and only one supply of water required the whole time it is in use."

Extract from POULTRY *May 4th, 1883.*

" Your machine is one I could recommend to anybody. I had 35 live chicks last month from 40 eggs. — *Mrs. Early, Newland, Witney, Oxon, Jan. 25, 1885.*

OPINIONS OF THE PRESS.

" We found when testing the machine. that it kept its heat very even indeed, and with as much regularity as any lamp machine we have tried."- FANCIERS' CHRONICLE. *May 30, 1879.*

" The merits of this Incubator are its size, the simplicity of its working, its capital regulator, its excellent arrangements for air and moisture, and the small cost of oil it burns."—PRACTICAL ARTIFICIAL INCUBATION, *by Edward Brown, Esq.. Messrs. Cassell, Petter & Galpin.*

" It is evident enough that the practice of 'filling up' from time to time as eggs are laid and there is room *does not answer* for at least Hydro Incubators. On the other hand it is remarkable that Cashmore's Lamp Incubator seems to have stood this particuar ordeal of 'filling up' remarkably well."—LIVE STOCK JOURNAL, *July 30, 1880.*

Our stock of these Incubators having been disposed of previous Price Lists are hereby cancelled. As proof that good materials are used, and good workmanship employed, we have only received for repairs, during our long connection, two Incubators affected with leakage, and both these were the result of accident ; in oue the connection between the funnel and cistern, and in the other between the tap nipple and cistern were broken.   We now guard against the recurrence of these accidents, by riveting as well as soldering the joints, and have every reason to believe that with ordinary care our machines will last a lifetime.

Patent ✢ Automatic ✦ Incubator.

No. 2.

These Incubators are well and substantially made, cases of best seasoned pine, stained and varnished, fittings lacquered brass, fitted with our new anti-moisture arrangements, are unaffected by barometrical or hygrometrical influences, and are far ahead of any other machine—our No. 4 and 5 excepted.

Will be found useful as auxiliary machines, and will meet the requirements of those fanciers, who desire a cheap Incubator.

Price, to hold 50 Eggs, Galvanized Iron Cistern ... £3 0 0
   ,,   ,,   ,,   ,,   Copper Cistern 3 15 0
   ,,   ,,   100   ,,   Galvanized Iron Cistern ...   4 10 0
   ,,   ,,   ,,   ,,   Copper Cistern 5 12 0

Incubator No. 3, as above, but fitted with stationary Lamp for
   Paraffin or Gas, as Illustration No. 5, 10/- extra to order.

Patent ✤ Automatic ✤ Incubator,

No. 4.

The only thermostatic Incubator in the world, unaffected by barometrical, hygrometrical, or external thermal
variations; can be worked successfully during any weather.
in any room, between, and including, a canvas tent and a
conservatory. Chicks dried up, glued in the shell, dead in
the shell, deformed feet, etc. are things of the past. Any
child who can be trusted to trim a lamp can work this
successfully. Superior make and finish in every way as No. 2.

PRICES AS UNDER—

30 Egg,	Copper Cistern,	£5	Galvanized Iron Cistern,	£4
60 ,,	,, ,,	7	,, ,, ,,	6
120 ,,	,, ,,	10	,, ,, ,,	8

Incubator No. 4, fitted with Stand, as per Illustration
No. 5, Price 5/- each extra.

Patent ✦ Automatic ✦ Incubator,

No. 5.

The temperature is ascertained by a thermometer in the tank, and is also fitted with our anti-moisture arrangements, as No. 4. but these are not shown in illustration.

Fitted with Stand, Gas, and Paraffin Lamp arrangements.

PRICES AS UNDER—

30 Egg, Copper Cistern, £5 15s.			Galvanized Iron Cistern £4 15s				
60 „	„	„	7 15	„	„	„	6 15
120 „	„	„	10 15	„	„	„	8 15

Old Pattern Brooder.

To accommodate 50 Chicks £1   10   0

„   „   100   „   2   0   0

These will be found useful as drying boxes, but are not absolutely necessary. Owing to the probability that a large number of unregulated and thermostat-in-the-incubator machines will very soon be thrown out of work, and may be purchased as "drying boxes" at a cheap rate, these Brooders will only be made to order.

The New Brooder.

The New Brooder utilizes the animal heat generated by the young birds themselves, and only a genial warmth is necessary for successful rearing. Having neither lamp nor hot water they are well adapted for use in a greenhouse, which need not be overheated for the purpose. In mild weather they may be used in a Poultry-house, or in the open, and will need no artificial warmth whatever, if the temperature is as high as 40 deg. Fahr. during the first week, after this a few degs. lower will do no harm. They are constructed in sets, which nest one in another, and as the chickens grow the smaller ones are removed to give the necessary room. A set can take charge of all the chicks which can be hatched in the corresponding incubator, and brood them up to six weeks old. For the idea of this Brooder we are indebted to the honey bee and the economy of the hive. We had such confidence in chicks keeping themselves warm in a properly constructed Brooder (Hive), that we trusted 62 chicks to themselves and Brooder on the 28th of April, 1890, which were hatched in our Incubator only two days previous, and our faith was rewarded by seeing the whole lot (except three which were killed by accident) reared most successfully in a spare greenhouse, without any artificial heat whatever ; after this we trusted other chicks as soon as they were hatched with like results, and we certainly shall never use a heated Brooder again. These are well made of best pine, varnished, dovetailed, grooved and tongued.

Price per Set of 4, No. 1 (25 to 80 chicks) ... £1 10 0

  ,,   ,,   ,,   ,, ,, 2 (50 to 60 ,,) ... 2 5 0

Section of Rearing House.

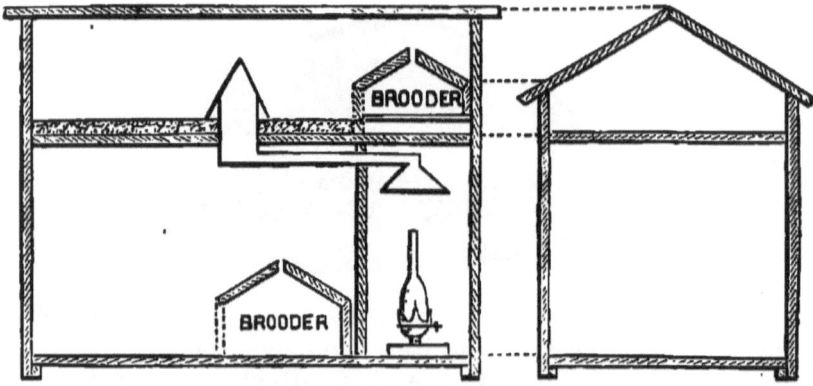

For Poultry Breeders who have not a suitable house at command these will be found very handy for rearing quantities, such as one or two Incubators can hatch, and the Lamp will carry the chicks through the most unfavourable weather. In warm weather the Lamp need not be lighted. The object, as will be seen, is to keep the severe weather from the run ; the chicks provide their own fuel when nesting in the Brooder. They are made in sections, and can be taken to pieces or put together in a few minutes by a handy man. They are substantially made, with part glass roof, painted three coats.

PRICES AS UNDER—
No. 1, 2-ft. 3-in. wide, 4-ft. long, 3-ft. 9-in. high ... £3 10 0
,, 2, 3-ft. wide   6-ft. long, 4-ft. 9-in. high ... 5 10 0
BROODERS EXTRA.

No. 2 Brooder can be used with No. 1 Rearing-house, but it is not advisable to crowd.

Drawings and Specifications for large Rearing-houses, heated by slow combustion stoves and circulating pipes supplied at a reasonable charge, and quotations given for the construction of same.

Prices quoted are for cash, with order, or on receipt of priced invoice. Our low prices do not allow sufficient margin for credit, or expense of collection.

The drawer of all our Incubators, except the 30 egg size, can be altered by a simple arrangement to hold goose eggs. All Incubators are tested before being sent out, and are made in the best manner possible. Cases of best pine stained (walnut) and varnished, having highly finished brass mountings. With ordinary care they will last a lifetime.

All goods are packed and put on Midland, or London and North Western Railways free. Packing cases to be returned.

IMPORTANT ANNOUNCEMENT!

WHOLESALE

HATCHING ✣ COMPETITIONS.

Fanciers, wishing to compare the quality and percentage of chicks hatched in these Improved Incubators, with those hatched in any other machine, or under hens, can have eggs hatched at 3d. each.

CONDITIONS.

Thirty or sixty eggs to be sent, carriage paid, together with a deposit of 7/6 or 15/-. The name of sender to be written upon each egg, commencing at or near one end and writing towards the other.

On my part I undertake to return the chicks safely packed, together with *the shells they came out of*, unhatched eggs, if any, and change.

Should a fair percentage of the eggs prove fertile, 3d each will be charged for chicks produced and change will be returned for unhatched eggs.

Should none, or only a very small number prove fertile, 1/- will be deducted to cover expenses incurred, and the balance will be returned with the eggs.

All eggs broken or spoilt, through accident or carelessness on our part, will be paid for at the rate of 3d. each over and above the 3d. deposited. Ladies or gentlemen availing themselves of this offer should make arrangements before sending eggs, as only a limited number of machines can be used for this purpose.

The sender or his agent may at any time between 7 a.m. and 10 p.m. inspect the eggs and see that they are under *artificial* incubation. If anyone can shew how I can possibly cheat in these competitions, I shall be pleased if they will suggest further safeguards.

www.ingramcontent.com/pod-product-compliance
Lightning Source LLC
Chambersburg PA
CBHW022156020726
47496CB00008B/2745